Sylvester was a
big, tough croc.

So was Arnold.

SYLVESTER & ARNOLD

BY DAVID BEDFORD
ILLUSTRATED BY TOM JELLETT

LITTLE HARE
www.littleharebooks.com

For all the big, tough crocs —DB
For Tom and Ruby —TJ

Little Hare Books
an imprint of
Hardie Grant Egmont
Ground Floor, Building 1, 658 Church Street
Richmond, Victoria 3121, Australia

www.littleharebooks.com

First published 2013
First published in paperback 2013

Cataloguing-in-Publication details are available
from the National Library of Australia

978 1 742 975 35 1 (pbk)

Designed by Vida & Luke Kelly
Produced by Pica Digital, Singapore
Printed through Asia Pacific Offset
Printed in Shen Zhen,
Guangdong Province, China,
December 2012

5 4 3 2 1

The illustrations in this book were
created with a combination
of brush-and-ink and
digital rendering.

Sylvester wore tough-croc shorts,
a tough-croc vest and tough-croc boots.
When he went out to play,
he put on an ugly, tough-croc face.

So did Arnold.

Sylvester spent all day making sure everyone knew how tough he was.

He snapped branches in his jaws and chased small animals for fun.

So did Arnold.

The swamp was big and wide,
and Sylvester and Arnold had never met.

Until one day ...

They **bumped** into each other.

Sylvester **bared his teeth**. So did Arnold.

Sylvester made his **eyes look bulgy**. So did Arnold.

Sylvester grabbed Arnold with his
favourite two-claw grip.

He got ready to throw Arnold
over his shoulder.

Arnold grabbed Sylvester with **his favourite two-claw grip.**

He got ready to knock Sylvester sideways with a swipe of his tail.

But suddenly they heard a loud **hiss . . .**

It was an **ENORMOUS** croc.

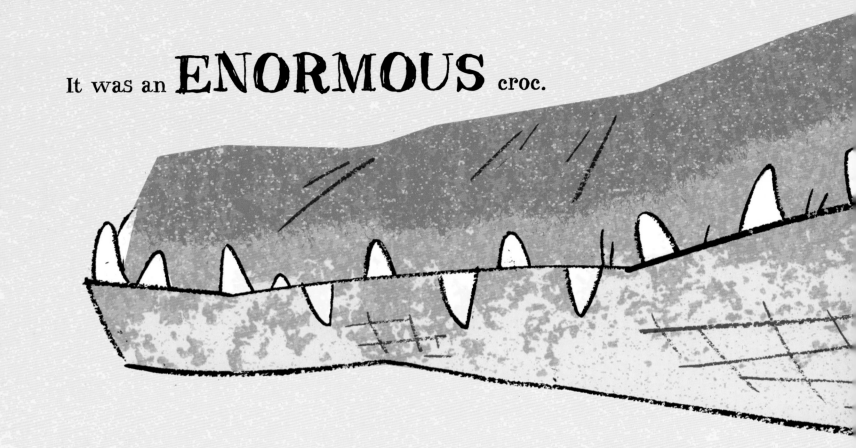

She had the **ugliest** tough-croc face
and **bulgiest** tough-croc eyes
Sylvester and Arnold had ever seen.

'I'm called Betty,'
she roared. 'Betty the Bad!

I'm moving in to this swamp!
And I'm so big and tough,
no one can stop me!'

Betty grabbed Sylvester and Arnold in a
GIGANTIC two-claw grip.

Then ...

Sylvester and Arnold landed in the deepest, slimiest, boggiest hole in the swamp.

They watched Betty the Bad
snapping whole trees,
chasing away the other animals,
and messing up their toys.

'This is my swamp now,'
she bellowed.

Sylvester and Arnold didn't feel like
big, tough crocs anymore.

'I'm going to find a new swamp
to live in,' said Sylvester. 'So am I,' said Arnold.

Sylvester and Arnold didn't dare to move
until it was dark.

'I'm scared that Betty will see us,' said Sylvester.

'So am I,' said Arnold.

Sylvester held Arnold with his favourite
two-claw grip, to help him feel safer.

Arnold held Sylvester with his favourite
two-claw grip, to help him feel braver.

Then they set off
to find new swamps.

Betty watched something creeping from the **slimiest**, **boggiest** hole in the swamp.

'Whatever that is, I'm going to scare it away,' she said.

But when she tiptoed closer, she saw ...

two shaking heads with **rattling teeth**...

four staring eyes... eight gripping claws...

and **two hard,** knobbly tails.

It was the **scariest** thing Betty had ever seen.

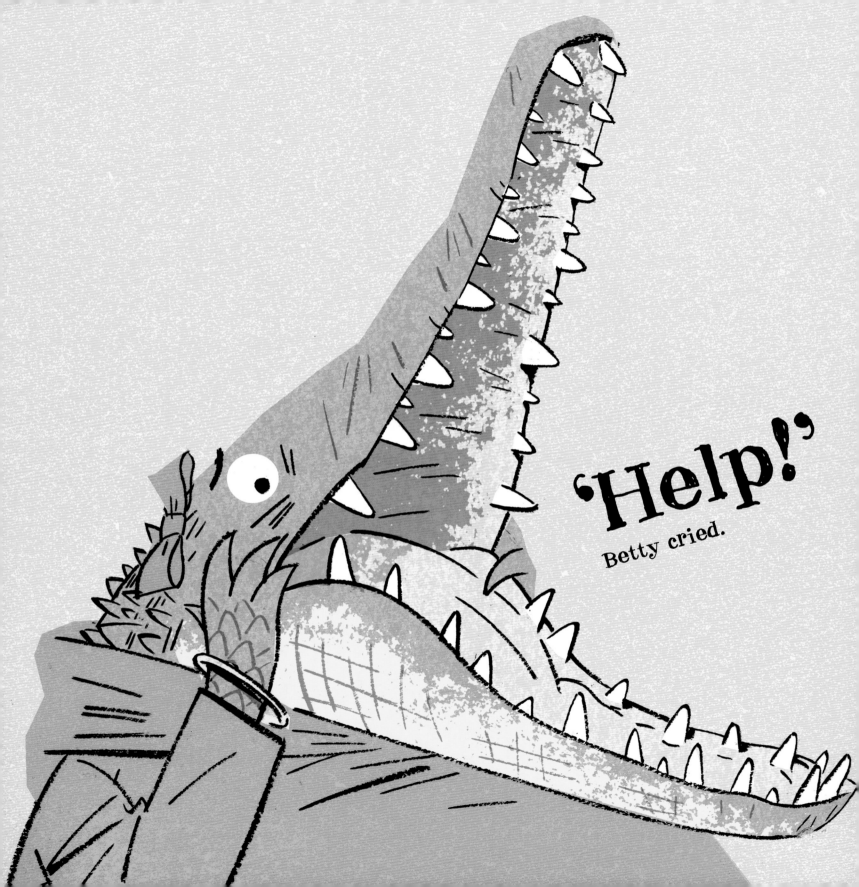

'Help!'

Betty cried.

Betty didn't look like a
big, tough croc anymore.

Sylvester looked at Arnold.

Arnold looked at Sylvester.

Then they reached out with their two-claw grips
and helped Betty climb out of the boggy hole.

After that ...

Sylvester was still a big, tough croc.

He wore tough-croc shorts,
a tough-croc vest and tough-croc boots.

But when he went out to play, he always had a
happy, friendly-croc face.

So did his new **best friends,**
Betty and Arnold.